Diamond Place

HART'S CROSSING SERIES #3

ROBIN LEE HATCHER

Revell

Grand Rapids, Michigan

Published by Fleming H. Revell
a division of Baker Publishing Group
P.O. Box 6287, Grand Rapids, MI 49516-6287
www.revellbooks.com

Printed in the United States of America

Library of Congress Cataloging-in-Publication Data
Hatcher, Robin Lee.
    Diamond Place / Robin Lee Hatcher.
        p.   cm. — (Hart's Crossing series ; #3)
    ISBN 10: 0-8007-1856-9 (cloth)
    ISBN 978-0-8007-1856-5 (cloth)
    1. Teenage girls—Fiction. 2. Pitchers (Baseball)—Fiction.
  3. Divorced mothers—Fiction. I. Title.
PS3558.A73574D53 2006
813'.54—dc22   2005033791

To Ian, Shayla, Vince, Xavierre, Sitarra, and Salvatore
Almost a baseball team of our own

1

Lyssa Sampson stared at her reflection in the bedroom mirror as she gave the brim of her baseball cap a slight tug. She did her best not to show any emotion. *Baseball Digest* said that's how Cardinal pitcher Chris Carpenter did it. The article, found in one of her older issues of the magazine, said concrete budged more easily than Carpenter's face. It called him "the Lord of Bored." That's how Lyssa wanted to look when she stood on the pitcher's mound.

"Lyssa," her mom called from downstairs. "Are you getting dressed?"

"Yeah."

"Well, hurry up. Your breakfast is about ready."

"Okay. Just a minute."

Lyssa removed the baseball cap and slipped it into her backpack along with her schoolwork and books. After a moment's hesitation, she shoved a couple issues of *Baseball Digest* into the backpack, too. She needed to memorize a few more stats before the next practice. She wanted Coach Jenkins to know she was serious about baseball.

Real serious.

"Lyssa!" Terri walked to the foot of the stairs and looked up toward her daughter's bedroom. "Your breakfast is ready now. Hurry up or you'll be late for school."

"Comin', Mom."

Terri returned to the kitchen, where she scooped fluffy scrambled eggs onto a plate. She heard the telltale sound of her ten-year-old daughter's imminent arrival—athletic shoes stomping hard on the steps as Lyssa took the stairs two at a time. Moments later, Lyssa entered the kitchen, backpack slung over one shoulder.

"Do you have your homework with you?" Terri asked.

"Yeah."

She lifted an eyebrow and gave her daughter a hard look. "Are you sure? I don't want to have to leave the salon like I did yesterday to bring your papers to the school."

"I've *got* it, Mom." Lyssa dropped her backpack onto the floor, then slipped onto a bar stool at the kitchen counter.

Terri turned to the stove, added two strips of bacon and a slice of buttered toast to the plate, and slid it across the counter. Lyssa took her fork and began shoveling eggs into her mouth as if it had been a week since her last meal.

"Slow down, honey."

Lyssa swallowed and grinned. "You told me I was gonna be late. I'm just doin' what you said."

Terri leaned her backside against the edge of the sink. She took enormous pleasure in her daughter. Watching her eat, watching her sleep, watching her play baseball—it all brought pleasure. Of all the blessings in Terri's life, Lyssa was the greatest.

Without looking up, her daughter said, "Don't

forget you're gonna bake your special cake for the Cavaliers' carnival tomorrow night."

Terri winced. She had forgotten. Not the fundraiser itself, but that she'd volunteered to bring a cake. Why hadn't she written it in her day planner when she volunteered? She knew better than to trust things like that to memory. Her schedule and Lyssa's schedule were jam-packed during the school year. Without her list of "to do's," Terri was lost.

She would be the first to admit that it wasn't easy being a single parent with no other family to lend support. Some days she felt stretched to her absolute limit. Thankfully, she had many friends in Hart's Crossing and a wonderful church family who stepped in to help when needed.

She turned toward the recipe box, flipping open the lid with her left hand while reaching for a shopping list and pen with her right.

"Coach Jenkins says I'm pitching really good. Maybe he'll let me be a starting pitcher at least once this summer. Wouldn't that be something? First girl to start a game in the major division of the Cavaliers."

"Yes, it would be something." Terri had enough

flour, but she would need more sugar and eggs. She scribbled on the notepad. "But remember, all the pitchers on your team are a year or two older than you are. You can't count on starting a game."

Lyssa laughed. "I'm a whole lot better than Bobby Danvers, and he's twelve."

"Pride goes before a fall, young lady."

"Huh?"

"I mean, you still have a lot to learn. Don't think you know it all."

"I don't think that."

Terri frowned as she stared at the notepad. Oh, yes. She needed two packages of frozen cherries, some unsweetened cocoa, and a carton of whipping cream. She would shop for groceries on the way home from work today and bake the black forest cake first thing in the morning before heading to the salon for her Saturday appointments.

"Mom? Did you hear me?"

Terri turned around. "I'm sorry, honey. What did you say?"

"I'm going now." Lyssa stood beside the kitchen

stool, once again holding her backpack. "See you after school."

"Not without a kiss, you don't." She stepped forward and brushed her lips across her daughter's forehead. "And put your coat on. It's cold, and that sweatshirt isn't enough to keep you warm."

Lyssa rolled her eyes but obediently headed for the rack beside the back door.

Moments later, alone in the kitchen, Terri completed writing her shopping list, set it on top of her planner, then went upstairs to dress for work. She chose jeans, a rust-colored sweater with three-quarter sleeves, and—the most important item for a person who was on her feet all day—comfortable shoes. With a quick glance in the mirror, she determined a ponytail would have to do. No time for fussing with her hair.

She smiled ruefully at her reflection. *Good thing my clients don't judge my expertise based on how I look.*

It was a short drive from her home on the west side of Hart's Crossing to Terri's Tangles Beauty Salon, located at the corner of Main and Municipal. The car's heater didn't have time to take the chill out of the February air before she pulled her 1991 Toyota Camry into the reserved spot near the back of the shop.

"Brrr."

She rushed to the entrance, shoved her key in the lock, and pushed open the door. Before she had time to do more than shrug out of her coat, the telephone rang.

She lifted the receiver from the back room's wall phone. "Good morning. Terri's Tangles."

"Hey, Terri. It's Angie. Got a minute?"

Terri moved toward the coffeemaker, pressing the handset between shoulder and ear. "Sure. My first client isn't due for about forty-five minutes. What's up?"

"I wanted to see what you're doing on May 20th about 2:00 in the afternoon. It's a Saturday."

"I don't have any clients booked out that far." She filled the carafe with cold water and poured it into the reservoir. "You can pick whatever time you want. Hang on. Let me get my appointment book, and I'll—"

"I don't need an appointment for my hair, Terri. I need a maid of honor and a flower girl."

For an instant, Terri froze in place. Then she squealed. "Are you teasing me, Angie Hunter? Because if you are, so help me, I'll—"

"I'm not teasing. Last night, Bill asked me to marry him."

"It's about time." Terri couldn't think of better news. Bill Palmer and Angie Hunter were two of her favorite people, and she thought them perfect for each other. She'd been hoping and praying for this to happen for months and months. "I was wondering when Bill would get off his keister and propose. Sometimes that man is as slow as molasses."

Angie laughed.

"Did he give you a ring?"

"Yes. He did the whole routine. Candlelight dinner. Soft music playing in the background. He even got down on one knee to propose. When I said yes, he slipped the engagement ring on my finger. It was very romantic."

Terri sighed. "I'm sure it was. Bill's a romantic kind of guy."

"Mmm."

"Can you swing by the salon today? I'd love to see the ring and give you a hug. I'll be here until 3:00."

"Sure, I'll drop by. And you and Lyssa will be my maid of honor and flower girl, won't you?"

"Of course. As long as you don't make us wear something too atrocious or froufrou."

The two of them laughed in unison before exchanging a few words of farewell. Moments later, Terri hung up the phone and returned to the coffeemaker.

Angie, Bill, and a May wedding. How delightful. She wondered if they planned to be married in the church or outdoors. May weather could be iffy, but the gazebo in the park was a wonderful location for a wedding.

Terri and her ex-husband, Vic, had been married by a justice of the peace in Twin Falls. Neither of them had any family in Hart's Crossing—Terri's parents were deceased and Vic's family all lived back East—and he hadn't wanted to wait to plan a more formal wedding. At the time, Terri had thought it romantic that he was in such a hurry to become her husband, but she should have wondered instead about his impatient nature. His spur-of-the-moment decisions had caused her much grief.

More than seven years had passed since Vic Sampson left town with that blonde he met at the ski resort—not the first woman he'd flirted with during his marriage to Terri, but the only one who'd convinced him to leave his wife and get a divorce.

Terri's love for her ex-husband had long since died, but time couldn't completely heal the wounds of a failed marriage. She'd never planned to be a divorced mom. She'd never wanted her daughter to grow up without a father. But that's what happened anyway.

Terri gave her head a quick shake. Let sleeping dogs lie. That's water under the bridge. No crying over spilt milk. Pick a cliché. They were all true. Dwelling on the past couldn't change it.

Once, Angie had asked her if she was interested in marrying again. Terri had answered, "I hope I can find the right guy, the one God means for me to marry. One day I hope Prince Charming will ride into town and sweep me off my feet."

So far Terri had seen neither hide nor hair of a tall, dark, and handsome prince and his white horse galloping down Main Street.

"Hey, Coach Jenkins." Lyssa smiled at her Little League coach, who was standing in the hall outside the school office. "Whatcha doin' here?"

"Morning, Lyssa." He nudged his glasses with the knuckle of his right index finger, then winked at her. "I've been called to the principal's office."

Lyssa liked the coach, but sometimes he was kinda weird. Even she knew the principal couldn't call just anybody to her office, not somebody who didn't have kids in the school, anyway. The coach didn't have kids or a wife.

"Are you ready for the carnival tomorrow night?" he asked. "We've got lots of money to raise for the Cavaliers."

"Uh-huh. I'm ready." She tried to stand a little taller, appear a little older, maybe not look so much like a girl and more like a pitcher. "My mom's gonna make her special chocolate cake for the cakewalk. It's really good."

"Terrific. I love chocolate cake. Maybe I'll win it."

The bell rang, announcing time for students to get to their classrooms.

"I better go, Coach. See you tomorrow night."

"See you there. And tell your mom I'm looking forward to trying out that cake of hers."

"Okay."

Lyssa suppressed a sigh as she walked away. What was she doing, talking about cake when what she wanted was to make the coach realize she was as good a pitcher as any of the boys on the team? Maybe she was only ten, and maybe they'd never had a girl pitcher before, but she oughta get a chance.

She should have quoted some of those stats she'd memorized or talked about the Little League teams that played in last year's World Series or even told him how often she practiced.

And tell your mom I'm looking forward to trying out that cake of hers.

Her brow puckered. Sure would be nice if he'd said something about her pitching arm or her fastball instead of her mom's cake, even if Lyssa was the one who'd brought it up first. Of course, if the coach really liked chocolate cake all that much, and he got her mom's and thought it was good, maybe he would notice Lyssa a little more. And if he noticed her a little more, then maybe . . .

Hmm. That gave her an idea.

2

Mel Jenkins arrived later than he'd anticipated at Hart's Crossing Community Church, site of the Cavaliers' final fund-raiser before opening day. By the time he entered the church's basement, where the carnival would be held, volunteers had finished stringing crepe paper across the ceiling and tying helium-filled balloons to whatever would hold them. Brightly colored booths—darts, fishing for prizes, ping-pong balls to win goldfish, even a pie-throwing booth—were set up on two sides of the room. In the opposite corner from where he stood, volunteers prepared for the cakewalk.

He shucked off his coat, tossed it onto a nearby folding chair, and rolled up his shirtsleeves. Then he looked for someone to tell him where his help was most needed.

Mel was a relative newcomer to Hart's Crossing—five years, which wasn't long in a small town like this—and he still felt like an outsider. But that was his own fault. He'd kept to himself after moving here from Montana. His relocation had come after he accepted a position as manager of a local bank. At the time, all he'd wanted was to be left alone with his memories and his grief—and his anger at God for taking Rhonda, his fiancée, from him.

Time had helped ease his sorrow, and finally he'd opened the door to let God into his heart to complete the healing. Becoming the coach of the Hart's Crossing Cavaliers was one step he'd taken to become a part of the community, another way to remind himself that he was among the living.

"Hey, Coach."

He turned his head. "Hey, Lyssa."

Mel liked the Sampson girl. Charming and funny, talented and determined, she had as much potential as any other player on the team. More potential than most, actually. One of only three ten-year-olds on the team, she needed a bit more experience as well as some time to grow. He figured the Cavaliers were in for a winning season and that Lyssa would play an important part in it, even if this was her first year in the major division.

"Wanna come help blow up balloons for the dart booth? It's takin' forever to get enough of 'em ready. That's where I'm headed."

"Sure, I'll help."

Strawberry-blond braids bouncing against her back, Lyssa led the way across the room to a purple booth. When she reached it, she stopped and looked over her shoulder. "You remember my mom, don't you?"

It wasn't until then that Mel saw the woman seated on the floor inside the booth, a half-blown balloon stuck between pursed lips. "Nice to see you, Mrs. Sampson."

Cheeks red, eyes narrowed, Terri exhaled forcefully, then took the balloon from her mouth and tied a quick knot in the end. "Thanks," she said once she caught her breath. "Nice to see you, too." She held out a package of new balloons. "Be my guest."

"Here's a chair, Coach Jenkins." Lyssa shoved the metal folding chair up against the back of his legs.

He sat on it at the same moment Terri rose from the floor. He'd have to say that this was the first time he'd noticed how pretty Lyssa's mom was. Of course, the other times he'd seen her had been at Little League organizational meetings, and she'd sat in the back of the audience while he stood in front of the group. They'd never had the opportunity to talk one-on-one.

She had unusual eyes, he thought now that he was close enough to see them. Not quite green. Not really blue. Striking with her red hair, too. Unusual. Almost like—

Suddenly aware that he was staring at her—and also aware that she *knew* it—he lowered his gaze to the bag of balloons in his right hand. "Guess I'd better get to work."

It had been a long time since he'd noticed the color of a woman's eyes or hair. Doing so now surprised him.

In the first couple of years after Rhonda's death, he'd been numb to everything. After that, he'd put up an invisible shield whenever he was around women, not willing to risk an involvement that might later cause him heartache.

So when had he lowered that protective shield?

"Coach, don't forget you're gonna try to win my mom's chocolate cake in the cakewalk tonight."

"What?" He looked at Lyssa. "Oh. Sure. You bet."

A man hadn't been tongue-tied in Terri's presence in ages. If Mel Jenkins was always this flustered around women, it would explain why he was a bachelor at his age.

She subdued a smile and put another balloon between her lips before casting a surreptitious glance in Mel's direction. He was a man of good looks, medium height, and muscular build. The creases between his eyebrows and the slight squint of his blue eyes made her wonder if the prescription for his eyeglasses needed adjustment. He had pale blond hair and fair skin that probably required 45 SPF sunblock lotion. As a redhead who burned easily, she sympathized.

Terri didn't know much about the coach other

than that he managed one of the two banks in town, had moved to Hart's Crossing from somewhere in Montana, and was enthusiastic about Little League baseball. Most gossip eventually spilled into Terri's salon, but nothing of significance had reached her ears about Mel Jenkins. Folks said he was friendly but reserved. Now she suspected extremely shy would be a better description.

Bill Palmer had recommended Mel for the coaching position when it became vacant. League rules called for a thorough background check of coaches and other volunteers, and Terri wouldn't have wanted it otherwise. Not the way things were these days. Still, it was Bill's endorsement that made her feel truly comfortable with Mel's involvement with Lyssa and the other kids on the team.

"How's it going here?"

Terri turned toward John Gunn, the pastor of Hart's Crossing Community Church. "Fine. We've got enough balloons ready to start tacking them to the board."

"Need more help?"

"I don't think so." She glanced at Mel. "Do we?"

He shook his head. "I think we can manage."

"We're doin' okay," Lyssa added before putting another balloon to her lips and breathing into it.

"I guess not," Terri said, looking at the pastor again.

"Good. Then I'll see who does need my help." With a wave, John moved toward the next booth.

Terri picked up a thumbtack before reaching into the large box of inflated balloons.

"Do you go to church here, Mrs. Sampson?" Mel asked after a brief period of silence.

"Please. Call me Terri." She poked a tack through the lip of a pink balloon and into the corkboard behind it. "Yes, this is my church. It has been since before Lyssa was born." She attached another balloon to the board. "What about you?"

"I attend services at the Methodist church over on Idaho Street. It's a small congregation, but I like it."

"I have a number of good friends who go there. Has Reverend Ball decided to retire yet?"

"No, not yet."

"He's talked about it for years."

"I've heard him say it, too, but I don't think he means it. Not yet."

Terri glanced over her shoulder. Although she was naturally attracted to tall, lean, dark-haired cowboy types, she conceded that Mel had a certain appeal, for a banker. Oh, and that dreadful haircut. Davis Wiggin, the local barber, must have cut it.

Now, if she could get her hands in Mel's pale hair, she would—

"Hey, Mom," Lyssa interrupted Terri's thoughts. "Mrs. Bedford's calling for you."

Terri felt heat rush to her cheeks, knowing she'd been caught staring, just as Mel had been caught earlier.

"I guess I'd better see what Patti wants," she said before hurrying away.

Patti Bedford, four months pregnant with her first child, stood near a table that held an array of beautiful cakes and pies, each covered with plastic wrap. She frowned down at a small, portable CD player.

"What's wrong, Patti?"

"Oh, this miserable thing won't work. I told Al

it was broken, but he insisted he'd fixed it." She looked at Terri. "I'd better run over to Radio Shack and buy a new one, or we may not have music for the cakewalk. Will you finish getting the numbers on the floor with the masking tape?"

"Sure. I'll get it done. And make certain you get a receipt so the league can reimburse you for the cost of the CD player."

"I don't know why Al thinks he can repair everything electrical." Patti reached for her coat and purse. "Sometimes he even puts the batteries into a flashlight backwards." She rolled her eyes. "Men."

Terri nodded as if in agreement, but she thought Patti was one of the fortunate ones. Al Bedford, young as he was, was a peach of a guy. He and Patti had been married almost two years, and he still hung on her every word, as if each one was made of pure gold. If Vic had treated Terri half as good . . .

Well, it was pointless for her thoughts to go there. Besides, it looked too much like envy for Terri's comfort. First Angie, now Patti.

"Shame on me," she muttered. "God has blessed me too much to envy others. Shame on me."

The coach kept blowing up and tying off balloons, one right after another, but Lyssa was pretty sure he'd watched her mom most of the time since she went over to the cakewalk area.

"Mom's cake's even better than it looks."

The coach turned his head. For a second, she thought he didn't understand what she'd said, but then he grinned. "Is that right? There looks like a lot of choices over there."

"Nope. Hers beats them all." Man, there she was, doing it again. Talking about her mom's cake when she could be impressing the coach with baseball stuff. She reached for another balloon while mentally scrambling for something better to say. Finally, it came to her. "Coach Jenkins, can you name the four pitchers who had twenty or more strikeouts in a single game?"

His eyes narrowed behind his glasses. "No, I don't think I can."

Lyssa grinned. "Tom Cheney of the Washington Senators had twenty-one back in 1962. Roger Clemens of the Boston Red Sox had twenty in two different games. One in 1986 and one in 1996.

Kerry Wood of the Chicago Cubs had twenty in—"
Uh-oh. What year was it? "Oh, yeah. That was in
1998. And the last one was Steve Carlton of the St.
Louis Cardinals. He had twenty in 1969."

"Mighty impressive, Miss Sampson."

She beamed. If those stats impressed him, just
wait until she—

"Hey, Jenkins. I could use your help."

Lyssa and the coach turned in unison to see Angie
Hunter and Bill Palmer standing beyond the booth's
front counter.

Not now! I was so close.

Bill motioned toward the stairs. "I've got cases
of soda pop to bring down. Can you give me a
hand?"

"Sure thing." The coach stood. "See you later,
Lyssa."

The two men strode away, leaving Lyssa with
baseball statistics racing through her head.

"Don't look so disappointed, squirt," Angie said.
"I'm staying."

"Sorry."

Angie settled onto the chair the coach had vacated

moments before. "Maybe you can help me decide on the colors I want to use at the wedding."

Like she cared about that when she could have been talking baseball with the coach.

Two hours later, the basement of the church was jam-packed with people. Voices buzzed and laughter rang as carnival-goers moved from booth to booth, happy to win silly prizes.

Terri greeted each person as she took their tickets for the cakewalk. "Thanks so much for coming tonight. . . . Hope you win a cake. . . . The Cavaliers appreciate your support. . . . Do enjoy yourself. . . ."

Till Hart, granddaughter of the town's founding father, approached Terri, a smile wreathing her face. Till never missed a community event if she could help it.

"Good evening, Miss Hart. Quite the crowd tonight."

"Always good to see folks turn out to support our youth." She offered Terri a ticket. "I hear you baked your famous black forest cake."

"I don't know how famous it is, but yes, I did."

"Well, that's the one I want to win. I've been thinking about it ever since Lyssa told me that's what you brought."

Terri looked over at the long table that held the desserts. At the end of it, Lyssa stood beside the brand-new CD player and a glass bowl full of numbers. "We're about to start a new walk, Miss Hart. You're the last one in for this round. Go stand on that empty number there." She pointed at the floor. "And good luck."

Till moved with surprising swiftness for someone her age. Sometimes Terri found it hard to believe the woman was really seventy-six.

I should be so spry. Which reminded her. She needed to be more faithful about riding the stationary bike she had in a corner of her bedroom.

Till Hart came to a standstill on the lone remaining number. She turned, looked at Terri, and winked.

Terri might have returned the wink, except her gaze was drawn to the man on the number in front of Till. It was Mel Jenkins. Terri didn't remember taking his ticket. How had he—

Music blared forth from the player, and Lyssa shouted, "Everybody walk. Follow the numbers. Everybody walk until the music stops."

"Step lively, Mr. Jenkins," Till said loudly as she passed by Terri. "I'm about to step on your heels. Men should never dawdle."

He responded, but Terri missed his words. However, she saw the teasing look in his eyes as he glanced back at the elderly woman following close behind him.

The music stopped abruptly. Participants shuffled forward or back to make certain each was standing on a number. Lyssa reached into the glass bowl and pulled out a slip of paper.

"Number fourteen. Who's on number fourteen?"

There was a moment of silence before Mel answered, "I am."

Lyssa dropped the paper back into the bowl. "All right, Coach! You get your pick." She pointed toward the black forest cake Terri had baked that morning. "That's the one you want."

Terri didn't miss the quick look he stole in her direction. "You promise it's the best one, Lyssa?"

"I promise. My mom made it."

The number on the slip of paper *could* have been fourteen. Of course, Lyssa would never know if it was or wasn't because she hadn't looked before dropping it back in the bowl. She'd sorta faked reading it.

Was it really lying if she didn't know for sure?

It wasn't like anybody spent a whole lot on those tickets anyway. Everybody came to the carnival to help raise money for the Little League, so win or not, they would've spent the same amount of money. Right?

3

Mel had been home from church a couple of hours when the telephone rang. Bill Palmer was on the other end of the line, calling in his official capacity as owner and editor of the *Mountain View Press*, the local weekly newspaper.

"Mind answering a few questions for the paper on your day off?" Bill asked after they'd exchanged a few pleasantries.

"No. Go ahead."

"Did the Cavaliers meet their financial objective last night? Would you call this year's carnival a success?"

Shifting the telephone receiver from his right ear to his left, Mel looked to the black forest cake in the center of his kitchen table. Eighteen hours after he'd brought it home, more than a third of it was missing. "Yes, on both counts."

"Coach Jenkins, it's not long now until the season opener. How do you think this year's team will fare?"

"We've got a strong bunch of experienced players. Most of them already have two years in the majors, and the rest have come up through the minors, many of them starting with Tee Ball. I think we'll see a winning season from this team."

Bill cleared his throat. "This is your first year as head coach of the Cavaliers. How are you feeling about the experience thus far?"

"It's been terrific. I like working with the kids, and the parents have really pitched in to help whenever and wherever they're needed. I've got no complaints. I hope they all feel the same way about me."

"Great." Bill chuckled. "Official interview over. Now tell me the truth. How's it going?"

"I *am* telling the truth."

Over the past year, he'd come to think of Bill as a trusted friend. They'd met at the local Chamber of

Commerce meetings when Mel first came to town, but it wasn't until last year that he'd been willing to be more than business acquaintances. He was thankful Bill wasn't the sort to be easily put off. The two men had plenty in common—never married, fortyish, interested in sports and current events, avid readers, Christians.

"The kids are great," Mel continued, "and so are the parents. We never lack for enough volunteers, no matter what needs done. I'm glad you talked me into coaching."

"Well, that's good to know. I'd hate to be responsible if you were miserable."

Mel reached for the cake in the center of the table and drew it toward him, recalling the pretty redhead who'd baked it. As quickly as the image popped into his head, he tried to shake it off by changing the subject. "Hey, I hear you've got a bit of news of your own. Something about you and Angie Hunter and a wedding."

"Man, that didn't take long to get around town. Who told you?"

"Betty Frazier was in the bank on Friday afternoon, checking about a loan for one of her real estate clients. I overheard her talking to a teller about the proposal."

Bill laughed again. "I don't know why I bother to publish a newspaper. Everybody knows everything before I can get the thing to press."

"True enough, but I promise to keep subscribing anyway."

"Thanks. I'll soon have a wife to support, so I've gotta sell lots of subscriptions."

A familiar heaviness weighed on Mel's heart as memories of Rhonda and what might have been pricked his thoughts. "You know I wish you and Angie the very best."

"Thanks."

"How about we meet for lunch or dinner later this week? That way I can get the straight facts instead of the gossip."

"Sure. What day?"

"Let me check my appointment schedule at the office, and I'll get back to you in the morning."

"Okay. Thanks for the comments for the paper."

"Not a problem. Be sure to remind folks to turn

out for the season opener." Rising from the chair, Mel said good-bye, then hung up the phone.

He turned, and his gaze swept over the kitchen. It was a room devoid of personality. Sterile, even. He'd bought the newly constructed house when he came to Hart's Crossing and lived in it for five years, but there was little evidence of that.

He looked at the black forest cake on the table. *I'll bet Terri Sampson's kitchen has plenty of personality.*

Maybe it was no accident that he'd noticed her green-blue eyes and the fiery color of her hair. He'd signed up to coach baseball as a reminder that he was among the living, but it might be time that the land of the living included more than his co-workers and a baseball team of ten-, eleven-, and twelve-year-olds.

Maybe it should include a woman, too.

Terri added another log to the fire, then returned to the couch, a soft blanket, comfy pillow, and the latest chick lit release from her favorite Christian author.

She loved lazy Sunday afternoons, especially in

winter. Sunday was the one day of the week when she allowed herself to be selfish, doing only things she wanted to do, activities that brought her pleasure. Today she didn't even mind the constant drum beat coming from the compact audio system in Lyssa's bedroom.

"Mmm." She scrunched down into a comfortable position and opened the novel.

Although cool weather would be around for several more weeks—according to Punxsutawney Phil and his shadow—there wouldn't be many more days that begged Terri to build a fire. Spring was almost upon them. Spring and baseball, followed by summer and baseball.

The telephone rang, but she made no move to answer it. Nine times out of ten these days, calls were for Lyssa. Shades of the teen years to come.

Terri shuddered. She was nowhere near ready to contemplate *that*.

"Mom! It's for you."

Glancing toward the stairs, she laid the book against her thigh. "Thanks, honey." She moved aside both book and blanket and rose from the sofa. "I need a cordless phone," she muttered as she walked into the kitchen and lifted the receiver. "Hello?"

"Mrs. Sampson? Terri. It's Mel . . . Mel Jenkins."

"Oh. Hello." She couldn't imagine why he might be calling. Other than last night's fund-raiser, Terri's volunteer duties for the Cavaliers didn't start until the season opener.

"Sorry to disturb you on a Sunday afternoon."

She cast a longing glance toward the living room couch. "No problem."

"I . . . uh . . . I wanted to tell you how delicious your cake is. The best I've ever eaten."

"Oh." She blinked. "Thank you."

"To tell you the truth, it's providing a bit too much temptation for one person. I'm afraid I'll eat the whole thing before the weekend's over."

Her brow puckered in a frown. Why on earth had he called to tell her that?

"Lyssa said this is her favorite cake, and I thought . . . Well, maybe I could bring some of it back to her. Unless, of course, you made two of them while you were at it."

"No, I didn't make two."

"Well, would you mind then? If I brought some of the cake over for Lyssa to enjoy?"

"I'm sure she would like that a lot—"

"Great. Why don't I bring it now? Unless that's an inconvenience."

Having discovered the previous evening how shy Mel was, Terri decided it wouldn't hurt to be kind to him. "No, it isn't an inconvenience. I'll let Lyssa know you're coming." She gave him directions to her house and then hung up the phone.

So much for an afternoon by the fire reading a good book.

A few moments later, she rapped on Lyssa's bedroom door, a knock that was drowned out by the pounding music. She opened the door, saying loudly, "Hey, honey. Turn that down, please."

Lyssa gave her a pained look but obeyed.

"That was your coach on the phone."

"Did we raise enough money?"

"I don't know. I didn't ask." Terri stepped into the bedroom. "But you can ask him yourself when he gets here. He's bringing over the cake he won last night."

44

Lyssa's eyes widened. "Didn't he like it?" Crestfallen, she sank onto the edge of her bed. "I thought he'd like it."

Terri chuckled. "Just the opposite. I think he liked it more than he should." She motioned with her head toward the door. "Come downstairs and give me a hand. He's on his way now."

"How could he like it more than he should?" Lyssa asked as she followed Terri.

"He said a whole cake is too much for just one person."

"Not *your* cake, Mom. I could eat it all by myself."

She laughed again. "True enough. But you don't have to think about your waistline the way adults do."

Mel parked his Ford F150 in the driveway of the Sampson home. It was a two-story house but not large. Just big enough for a divorced mother and one daughter. He wondered how long Lyssa's dad had been out of the picture. Did he see his daughter and ex-wife? Did he live in Hart's Crossing? Were they on good speaking terms? What if there was a chance of reconciliation? Mel didn't want to get in the middle of something like that.

Maybe coming here wasn't such a good idea. Terri Sampson was a friendly, attractive woman, but dating was difficult enough without outside complications. Maybe—

The front door flew open, and Lyssa appeared on the stoop. "Hey, Coach!" She waved an arm.

Good idea or not, it was too late to change his mind. He reached for the cake platter and got out of the truck.

"Mom said you couldn't eat that all by yourself."

He followed the sidewalk toward the front door. "Not quite what I said. I *could* have eaten it all, but I knew I shouldn't."

She gave him a look that said he was nuts. "C'mon. Mom's waiting."

As Mel stepped through the doorway into the living room, he noticed the blanket and book on the sofa and the dancing flames in the fireplace. Looked like he'd interrupted her plans. He shouldn't have come.

"Want me to take the cake?" Lyssa asked. "You can hang your coat in the closet there."

"Thanks." He handed her the platter, then shrugged out of his jacket.

Before he could open the closet door, he saw Terri step into the archway between living room and kitchen. She smiled in welcome, and the room seemed to grow brighter because of it.

Maybe this was a good idea after all.

Over cake and beverages—coffee for the adults and hot chocolate for Lyssa—the conversation turned quickly to Little League baseball. It was the one thing the three of them had in common, as far as Terri knew. Mel mentioned his hope for warmer weather by the season opener. Terri asked about the fund-raising results from the previous night. Lyssa announced she'd been working hard on her curveball.

"I'm proud of you, Lyssa," Mel said. "You've come a long way since team practice began."

Terri smiled, thankful that he took seriously her daughter's desire to improve. A few of the Cavalier team members gave Lyssa a hard time. She was the only girl in the major division and among the youngest of the Cavaliers. Some of the boys—and undoubtedly some of their parents—didn't think Lyssa belonged in the majors.

"Good enough to start a game next month?" Lyssa asked her coach, her voice filled with hope.

He gave a slight shake of his head. "This is your first year in the majors. This is the third year for both of our other pitchers, and they want to start as badly as you do. We'll have to see how the season goes. I'm not saying it won't happen. I'm saying we'll have to wait and see."

Terri noticed the way he looked directly at Lyssa as he spoke. His tone of voice was kind but firm. He didn't talk down to her daughter, as if her question was frivolous or unimportant.

Determination narrowed Lyssa's eyes. "Coach Jenkins, I'm gonna get good enough to start at least one game this year. You'll see."

"I hope you do, Lyssa."

Something warm blossomed in Terri's heart as she observed the two of them. A feeling so long unfelt she couldn't quite put a name to it.

4

Lyssa pushed open the door to the *Mountain View Press*. "Hey, Mr. Palmer. Mom said you wanted to see me."

"Yeah, I did." The newspaper editor rose from behind his cluttered desk. "Didn't expect you so soon though. I just talked to your mom half an hour ago."

"She had to run some errands after I got outta school, so she dropped me off on her way to the store."

Bill motioned her forward. "Come on back here. I ran across an old article from the Associated Press that I think you'll want to read." He picked up several sheets of paper. "After I read the first one, I searched out a few more on the Internet. Pretty interesting stuff. Did you hear about this girl when it happened?" He handed Lyssa the papers before sitting down again.

She recognized the name in the headline immediately. "Are you kidding, Mr. Palmer? *Everybody's* heard of Katie Brownell. She pitched a perfect game. She even got honored by the Baseball Hall of Fame."

The editor laughed softly. "So where was I when all that happened?"

"Dunno." She shrugged as she sat in a chair opposite him, then started reading the top article.

Katie Brownell is a shy 11-year-old girl of few words. But when she gets on the baseball field, she lets her pitching do the talking.

Brownell is the only girl in the Oakfield-Alabama Little League baseball program in this community about halfway between Buffalo and Rochester. On Saturday, that didn't stop her from accomplishing something league officials can't remember anybody—boy or girl—ever doing.

She threw a perfect game . . .

Wow, Lyssa thought. *Wouldn't that be something?*

And if Katie Brownell could do it, why couldn't she? She could if her coach believed in her enough.

Katie said she knew she had a chance for something special in the fourth inning. Fortunately, Katie's coach, Joe Sullivan, realized that, too.

He had intended to pull Katie at some point during the game and was ready to do it when the scorekeeper told him she had a no-hitter going . . .

"She's lucky she's got a coach who let her start a game and keep playing," Lyssa said.

"What's that?" Bill asked.

Lyssa looked up, only then realizing she'd spoken aloud. "Oh, nothin'."

He watched, waiting for her to say more, his eyes saying he knew she hadn't told him the whole truth. The look made her squirm inside. She hated it when adults did that, especially since it usually worked. She couldn't seem to keep her thoughts to herself.

She laid the papers in her lap. "I guess I'm jealous. I want what happened to her to happen to me."

"Who's to say it won't?" He smiled. "Your coach tells me you've got a great arm."

Strange. She'd felt pretty good about things yesterday when the coach came to her house and he sat at the table, talking with her and her mom. Lyssa had convinced herself she could prove to him she was good enough to start a game, even if she was only ten and a girl. Now it felt impossible. "Mr. Palmer, you can't pitch a perfect game if you don't get to *start* a game, and Coach Jenkins says I'm not ready to start one yet."

"I see." His expression grew serious. "Do you think maybe he's right?"

She looked down at the girl in the photograph in the article. "No," she muttered. "I'm ready."

"You know, Lyssa, the season hasn't even opened yet. Lots can happen in a couple months. That girl's perfect game was in May. Maybe by this May your coach will think you're ready."

"Yeah. Maybe." Lyssa slunk down in the chair. "It's just I want it so bad. Know what I mean? Have you ever wanted somethin' so bad it makes your insides hurt?"

He was silent a while before answering, "Yes. Believe it or not, Lyssa, I have."

The last errand on Terri's list was a visit to A to Z Arts and Crafts. She needed a new curtain for the back window at the salon. She hoped she could find fabric she liked and make the curtain herself. She wasn't much of a seamstress, but she could manage a curtain. A bit of cutting, a bit of hemming. Relatively simple.

She was browsing through the bolts of fabric when Francine Hunter, Angie's mother, appeared on the opposite side of the table.

"Oh, good. I'm glad I ran into you, Terri. I planned to call you as soon as I got home. The Thimbleberry Quilting Club is making a wedding quilt for Angie, and we hoped you'd want to participate. But it's a surprise. Don't say anything to her about it." As she spoke, she came around the end of the table.

"A quilt?" And Terri was hoping she could manage to sew a simple curtain.

"Well, we're not asking you to make an entire quilt, dear. Just one of the squares. Something that would be meaningful for Angie from you."

"I haven't done much needlework, Francine, but I'll do my best."

The older woman laughed softly. "Don't you worry. What I'm asking isn't nearly as difficult as you might think." She patted Terri's shoulder. "Trust me. The Thimbleberry gals will make sure you know what you're doing."

Terri wondered if she could bribe someone else to make her square in exchange for a perm or a haircut and color or even a French manicure.

"I don't know why we waited so long to get started," Francine said, oblivious to Terri's thoughts. "Everyone knew Bill would propose. Only the when was in question."

Terri smiled as she nodded in agreement. "He was smitten from the first moment he saw her after she returned to Idaho. He never stood a chance."

"So true." Francine paused and gave Terri a thoughtful look. "What we need now is to find a nice young man for you."

As if bidden by the woman's words, the image of Mel Jenkins sprang into Terri's mind. *"Nice" would certainly describe him,* she thought as she recalled the way he'd interacted with Lyssa yesterday. But Francine meant a love interest, and Terri wasn't attracted to Lyssa's Little League coach in that way.

Mel rounded the corner from Park onto Main in time to see Terri and Lyssa Sampson exit the offices of the *Mountain View Press*. Hand in hand, they crossed the street and disappeared into Terri's Tangles Beauty Salon. If he'd left the bank five minutes earlier, Mel would have met up with the mother and daughter. Too bad. He'd wanted to say how much he enjoyed his time with them.

He strode across the street, then followed the sidewalk to the brick building that housed the newspaper. When he opened the door, he caught a whiff of dust and newsprint. He wondered when the last time was that the office had been thoroughly cleaned. He knew he couldn't work amid all this clutter.

Not finding his friend in the front office, Mel called, "Hey, Bill. Are you back there?"

"I'm here." A few moments later, Bill appeared in the doorway to the print room.

"Would you mind going to eat a little earlier than we planned?"

"Not a bit. Let me grab my jacket."

A short while later, the two men sat in a booth at the Over the Rainbow Diner, the only restaurant in town, if one didn't count the Big Burger Drive-In, the Suds Bar and Grill, or the quaint tea shop Pearl Ingram opened last fall over near the senior center. They didn't talk as they perused the menu. In the end, they both ordered the baby back ribs special.

After the waitress left, Bill said, "Lyssa Sampson was in to see me not long before you came."

"I saw them leaving. Lyssa and her mom."

"I found an article about that girl who pitched a perfect game, and I showed it to her."

Mel suppressed a groan, knowing what reading about Brownell would do to Lyssa.

"I guess you don't think she's ready yet," Bill said as he loosened the paper napkin wrapped around his table service.

"Not yet. She will be, but not yet."

"She wants it bad."

Mel released a soft laugh. "Don't I know it." He

shrugged. "The good thing is, she plays hard even when she doesn't get what she wants. She never acts spoiled, the way some kids do."

"Lyssa isn't spoiled. Terri's done a good job raising her."

Mel tried to sound casual as he asked, "What about Lyssa's dad?"

"Vic Sampson?" Bill shook his head. "Who knows? He deserted the two of them years ago. Must be at least seven years by now. Never showed his face in Hart's Crossing again. He hasn't made any effort to stay in touch with his daughter."

"That's tough."

"I don't know how a man could do that to his family."

Mel glanced out the window. Clouds had drifted in from the west, turning the sky pewter in this last hour before sunset. "We live in a throwaway society. You don't want something, you chuck it."

"If there's anything I'm determined to do, it's to be a good husband to Angie, and if God blesses us with children, then a good father to them."

His friend's comment drew Mel's gaze from the

window. "You will be." The truth was, he envied Bill Palmer. Mel hadn't meant to be unmarried and childless at his age. He'd wanted a wife and kids, same as Bill.

Terri Sampson's pretty green-blue eyes flashed in his memory, the sound of her laughter lingering in his ears. He pictured Lyssa in her baseball uniform, her cap pulled low on her forehead, determination setting her mouth as she wound up to release the ball.

Maybe, God willing, it wasn't too late for him.

5

"I'm driving down to Twin Falls on Saturday morning to look at wedding gowns," Angie said as she settled onto the chair in front of the shampoo bowl. "Could you and Lyssa go with me? I'd love to see if we can find dresses for the two of you. Ones you'll like."

Terri shook her head as she eased Angie back against the neck rest. "I couldn't do it this Saturday. I've got several appointments scheduled, and Lyssa has baseball practice." She turned on the water and ran it until the temperature was right. "How about Monday afternoon, after Lyssa gets home from school? We could go then."

"Mmm. Let me think." Angie closed her eyes. "Yes, Monday will work for me."

Terri pressed down on the pump of the shampoo dispenser, then worked the golden liquid into Angie's dark brown hair.

"Oh, that feels heavenly."

"That's what I hear." Terri tried to remember the last time she'd had her scalp massaged by another hair stylist. Maybe back when she was in beauty school? Could it have been that long?

"Bill and I ordered the wedding invitations yesterday." Angie opened her eyes. "You know, it was kind of scary. Does that make sense? I love him and want to be his wife. Most of the time, I'm really excited. But it was still scary placing the order for those invitations. I guess it made it seem more real somehow. Am I crazy?"

Terri rinsed the shampoo from Angie's hair, sat her up, and wrapped her head in a towel before answering. "You're not crazy, Ang. It makes perfect sense. This is a big change in your life."

"Did you feel that way when you married Vic?"

"Not really." She shrugged and released a tiny

laugh. "I guess I didn't know enough to be nervous. We didn't have a long engagement or a fancy wedding. It all happened too fast for nerves or common sense to get in the way."

Angie rose from the chair. "I'm sorry," she said softly. "I didn't mean to bring up bad memories."

"Don't be silly. It's too long ago to hurt me now." Terri motioned for Angie to follow her to the styling chair. "Besides, whatever else Vic did wrong during our marriage, he did give me Lyssa, and I wouldn't trade her for anything."

No, she thought as she began trimming Angie's hair, she wouldn't trade Lyssa for anything, not even a happy marriage. But she wouldn't mind having both. She wished Vic had been a better man. She wished he'd been a Christian. She wished he'd wanted to be a husband to her and a father to Lyssa. And although memories of Vic didn't hurt any longer, she did sometimes wonder what was wrong with her that he'd felt the need to cheat.

"Bill and I want children," Angie said, interrupting Terri's thoughts. "I hope it's not too late for us."

Terri smiled at her friend in the mirror. "Women lots older than you are having babies, Ang. You're what? Thirty-six? I wouldn't worry if I were you."

The chime above the salon door rang. Before turning to see who'd come in, Terri cast a quick glance at the clock to make certain she wasn't running behind schedule. Thankfully, she wasn't.

"Hey, gorgeous."

Terri looked at Bill standing just inside the door. "Are you talking to me or my client?"

"Ah, I'm too smart to fall for that." He laughed. "You're both gorgeous. Ask any guy in town."

That was sweet of him to say, but it was obvious, as Bill gazed at Angie, who was truly beautiful in his eyes.

Okay. Terri might as well admit it. She would love to have a man look at her like that. Could it possibly be in God's plan to send someone her way who would?

Mel leaned back in the chair and swiveled it toward the window of his office. The vertical blinds were halfway open, enough to let in the daylight. If he opened them completely, he felt as if he were in a fishbowl because every passerby on the sidewalk could look right in.

Across the street, Dave Coble, the police chief, entered the post office moments before Harry Raney, owner of the Over the Rainbow Diner, came out the same door. Familiar sights. Familiar faces.

But the face that persisted in his thoughts belonged to one particular and very attractive redhead.

It was already Wednesday, and he still hadn't come up with another excuse to call Terri Sampson. There wasn't any more chocolate cake to share with her daughter, and he couldn't use Terri's involvement as a Little League volunteer too often. Of course, he *could* try the truth. He could tell her he liked her and wanted to invite her out to dinner or a movie. Or both.

He hated this feeling in his gut, all nerves and un-certainty. Normally, he was a confident guy, a fellow able to make decisions and then act on them. But the thought of asking Terri out made Mel nervous.

Through his twenties and into his early thirties, he'd had a number of girlfriends. He hadn't been what one would call a ladies' man, but he'd enjoyed the company of women. Then he'd met Rhonda, and he knew he was ready for that home in the suburbs with a jungle gym in the backyard and everything else that went with marriage and a family. After proposing, he'd thought his dating days were over for good.

But here he was again.

Mel shook his head slowly. He'd thought dating was like riding a bike. That one never forgot how. But it didn't seem to work that way. He felt more like a fifteen-year-old trying to stir up courage to ask a girl to the prom than a man hoping to enjoy an adult relationship with a woman.

His gaze moved to the telephone on his desk. Did he have the courage to take that next step?

Mel rose, walked to the window, and pulled the cord to open the vertical blinds wide. It was a gray and windy day, appropriate for the first of March, roaring in like a lion.

From the vantage point of his office, he could see up Park Street to the north. Main Street Drug was on the opposite corner from the bank and beyond the drugstore was Sawtooth Dentistry. To the south lay the offices of Randy Dickson, Attorney at Law, and the red brick First Baptist Church with its white steeple.

He'd come to like Hart's Crossing—and the people in it—over the years he'd lived here. At first it had been a place of escape, but it had grown on him. Somehow, despite himself, it had become home when he wasn't looking.

I don't have to feel empty and alone any longer. He raked the fingers of his right hand through his hair. *I can do something about it.*

He turned, strode to his desk, and yanked open the drawer where he kept the slim Hart's Crossing phone directory. He opened it, flipped through the pages to the *T*s, then followed his finger down the list until he arrived at Terri's Tangles Beauty Salon.

Drawing a deep breath, he picked up the handset and punched in the numbers.

Using the blow dryer with her right hand and a brush with the left, Terri had almost finished styling Angie's shorter hairdo when the salon's telephone rang.

What I wouldn't give for a receptionist. If I could afford to hire one.

She glanced toward Bill, who sat in the dryer chair, flipping through a magazine while he waited for his fiancée.

He'll have to do.

"Bill, would you mind getting that for me?" she asked above the whirr of the blow dryer.

"Sure thing." He got up and headed for the counter.

Catching Angie's gaze in the mirror, Terri asked, "Do you two have plans this afternoon? Or does he just need something to do?"

Angie laughed. "We've got plans. We're going to look at new living room furniture. The things I had in my place in California aren't right for Bill's house, and his furniture isn't fit for—"

Bill walked back into view. "That was Mel Jenkins. He asked you to call him at the bank. I wrote his number on the slip of paper by the phone."

Terri hoped Lyssa's coach didn't need her to volunteer for something else. One more thing on her calendar, and she would collapse.

She flipped the switch on the blow dryer, plunging the salon into sudden silence. "All done." She set the dryer in its slot. "What do you think?" As she swiveled the chair around, she gave Angie the hand mirror, then waited for the verdict.

"I like it."

Bill grinned. "Me, too."

Terri retrieved the hand mirror from Angie. "You should consider how you want to style your hair for the wedding. It could make a difference in the type of veil you choose. Or vice versa."

"Okay. I'll think about it. When we go to Twin, you can help me pick out a veil that'll work."

With the cape removed from around her neck, Angie rose and walked to the counter, where she wrote a check to pay for the cut and style. Then she and Bill said good-bye and left the salon, holding hands, their heads close together as they spoke softly to each other.

Terri sighed as she opened the register and slipped the check into the appropriate slot. As she closed the drawer, her gaze fell on the note Bill had scribbled.

She sighed again.

Might as well find out what Mel wanted. She just hoped she remembered how to say no if she needed to. She already felt as if she were running in three directions at once. Not that she didn't enjoy her volunteer work with the Cavaliers. She did. She had many friends among the other moms and dads, and she loved watching Lyssa play. Still, she wasn't Super Mom, despite how often she pretended otherwise.

Settling onto the stool behind the counter, she tapped the numbers and waited as the phone rang.

"Farmers Independent Bank. How may I direct your call?"

"Mel Jenkins, please."

"Certainly. May I tell him who's calling?"

"Terri Sampson."

"Oh. Hi, Terri. Didn't recognize your voice. It's Isabella."

Isabella . . . Isabella . . . Miranda Andrews' daughter? "Hi, Isabella. I didn't know you worked at the bank."

"Only part time. But I'm hoping I'll get to stay

68

on this summer after graduation. I'll need all the money I can save. I'm going to attend Boise State in the fall." The girl paused a moment before saying, "I'll put you through to Mr. Jenkins."

"Thanks."

Terri felt a twinge of envy. Wouldn't it be great to be in Isabella's shoes, eighteen years old with all of life still before her? Dorm rooms. Football games. Studying in the library. Pizza parties. Boyfriends. A girl with a clean slate, free of major mistakes.

Terri hadn't gone to college, and she often regretted it. Not that she'd had much choice. She hadn't had the money, and although her grades had been good in school, they hadn't been good enough to earn a scholarship.

"Mel Jenkins. May I help you?"

"Mel, it's Terri. You left a message for me to call." She pressed her lips together rather than asking what he needed. After all, he might have found some other volunteer already.

"Yes, I did." He cleared his throat.

Please don't let it be that he needs a driver for the van for away games. Anything but that.

69

"I was hoping to see you on Friday. Any chance you're free on such short notice?"

Relief flooded through her when she realized his call wasn't about the Little League. *Thank goodness.* She reached for her planner. "My last appointment is at 4:00. I could fit you in right after that."

"No. That wasn't what I meant." He half-chuckled, half-coughed. "I . . . uh . . . I wondered if you'd like to go to the movies with me. There's a *War of the Worlds* double feature playing at the Apollo. First the 1953 version, then the newer one. I've seen them both before. Lots of action and special effects. The Tom Cruise one's kind of gory but not too bad." He cleared his throat. "They aren't great movies, but they're what's playing."

It took Terri a moment to process his words. He was asking her out? On a date?

"I thought we could have dinner at the diner first."

Yes, he was definitely asking her out. Dinner and a movie was a date. She wasn't sure what to do. Mel was a nice, likable guy, but he was a banker, not a cowboy.

"Terri? Are you there?"

"Yes, I'm here."

"If you're busy right now"—obviously, he was giving her an out—"you could call me back later with your answer."

She opened her mouth, planning to decline his invitation, but surprised herself when she said, "No, I'm not busy, Mel. I'd like to see the movies with you."

"Great." He sounded pleased. "How about I pick you up at your house at 5:30?"

"That would be fine."

"See you Friday."

Terri returned the handset to its cradle. Talk about out of practice. It was almost a year since a man had asked her out, and that time she'd seen it coming long before it happened. Why had this invitation caught her off-guard?

She let the memory of her few encounters with Mel play through her mind, and for the life of her, she couldn't think of one instance—not even last Sunday when he'd brought the cake over to share with Lyssa—where he'd indicated a personal interest that might have prepared her.

What if she'd made a horrible mistake in agreeing? He was Lyssa's baseball coach. If Terri and Mel didn't get along, if their date was a complete bust, what would that mean for her daughter? Mel could make Lyssa's experience on the team miserable.

Terri pictured him in her mind again, sitting at her kitchen table, talking to Lyssa, and her worries eased.

6

"Mom! Mom, wake up!"

Terri heard Lyssa's voice through the mist of a dream. A dream she wasn't ready to leave.

"Mom!"

A hand shook her shoulder, and Terri came awake with a jolt. "Lyssa?" Her gaze shot to the digital clock at her bedside: 2:47 a.m. "What's wrong?"

"I'm scared." Lyssa lifted the covers and crawled into bed beside her mother.

"What is it, honey? Did you have a bad—" As she began to ask the question, she felt a blast of wind shake the house, giving her the answer. "It's storming, isn't it?" She put an arm around Lyssa's back and drew her close. "Well, don't worry. March

73

likes to come in with a lot of wind. We'll snuggle down under these blankets and get some sleep. By the time we wake up, it'll be over."

Her words were true for Lyssa, but sleep evaded Terri as the storm continued to batter the house, whistling around the eaves. A leafless tree danced eerily outside her bedroom window, the shadows cast upon the blinds by a nearby streetlight. Then the lightning began. A bright flash, followed by a crack of thunder. Another gust of wind. Another flash of lightning. More thunder. Again and again and again.

Terri hated storms like this one. They made the old place creak and moan. They made this small house feel fragile, and then Terri felt small and fragile, too. In the middle of a stormy night, she felt too alone, too frightened, too insignificant to handle what life tossed her way.

She glanced toward the clock. It was past 3:30. It seemed much more than an hour since Lyssa had awakened her.

Drawing a deep breath, Terri searched her mind for memorized words from Psalm 107, comforting words that she'd turned into a personal prayer for times such as this.

Father-God, you can still the storm to a whisper. You can hush the waves of the sea. I will be glad when it grows calm because I know you will guide me to my desired haven. Let me give thanks to you, Lord, for your unfailing love and your wonderful deeds for humankind. Let me exalt you in the assembly of the people and praise you in the council of the elders.

The fear in her heart receded as she silently repeated more words from the Psalms.

In peace I will lie down and sleep, for you alone, Lord, make me dwell in safety.

At last, the thunder moved into the distance, rolling across the heavens but no longer close and threatening. The gusting winds slowed. Raindrops began to rat-a-tat-tat against the window pane, a moment of warning before the skies opened in earnest.

Unlike wind, lightning, and thunder, Terri loved the sound of falling rain. She rolled onto her side, kissed Lyssa's forehead, and closed her eyes.

In peace I will lie down and sleep.

Perhaps she could find her way back to that lovely

dream. She didn't recall what it had been about, only that she'd felt happy in that misty playground of her mind at rest.

The doorbell rang. Once, then again.

Terri's heart felt as if it missed several beats as she sat up, tossing aside the blankets. She grabbed for her robe and rushed from the bedroom. A fist pounded on the door as she descended the stairs, alarming her even more.

She reached the door and jerked it open. Dave Coble stood on her stoop, his police hat and uniform covered with protective rain gear. "Dave?" She reminded herself that Lyssa was safe and asleep in the bed upstairs. "What is it? What's happened?"

"Sorry to get you up at this hour, Terri, but I thought you should know. That tree between your shop and the real estate office. The storm snapped it in two, and the top half came down on the roof of your building. Tore clean through." He jerked his head toward the rainy street. "I imagine things are getting mighty wet inside about now."

Her heart sank. "The salon's damaged?"

"Yes, ma'am." He put a hand on her shoulder.

"Nothing you can do until the rain stops, far as I can tell. Too slick to let anybody get up on the roof while it's still dark. Power's out over on that side of town. Something must've hit a transformer. Come first light you should be able to assess the damage."

Dawn was about three hours away. How much of the roof was gone? Would water destroy the inside of the salon? Shouldn't she go down there now and see for herself? No, she couldn't leave Lyssa all alone, and she couldn't wake her up and take her along; it was a school night. Besides, what could she do by herself anyway?

"I'd best be on my way, Terri. Sorry for waking you in the middle of the night with news like this, but I figured you'd want to know so you can get an early start."

"I'm glad you told me." She wasn't sure she meant that. A part of her would have preferred ignorance for a few more hours. Maybe she would have fallen back to sleep. She wouldn't sleep now, that was certain.

Dave Coble pinched the brim of his hat between index finger and thumb, gave a brief nod of his head, and turned to walk away. "'Night, Terri."

"Good night, Dave." With a sigh, she closed the front door.

Lord, how bad is it?

She had insurance on the building. Where had she put the policy? How much would it cover on the repairs?

O God, if I can't work, how can I take care of Lyssa? Where will the money come from?

As soon as Mel heard that a tree had fallen on Terri's building in the previous night's storm, he left the bank and walked down Main Street to see if he could be of help. He found Terri, Angie, and Bill standing on the sidewalk at the southwest corner of the salon. Angie's right arm was around Terri's shoulders in a comforting embrace, and from the look on Terri's face, she needed plenty of comfort.

"Morning, Mel," Bill said.

"Morning." He stopped beside the threesome. "I heard the storm did some damage." He turned and looked in the direction the others had been staring a short while before. *Oh, man.* The old gnarled tree that stood between the two buildings had snapped in two, the top crashing down on the roof of Terri's Tangles Beauty Salon.

Terri turned toward Angie and pressed her face into the curve of her friend's shoulder as she wept.

"Have you been inside yet?" Mel asked Bill softly.

"Not me, but Terri has."

"Come on. Let's have a look."

Bill glanced at his fiancée. "Wait here for us."

Angie nodded.

The two men walked away.

As soon as they were out of hearing, Mel said, "Is she okay?"

"Terri? She's pretty shaken up. She's worried about the insurance coverage and how soon she'll be able to return to work."

Mel opened the door and stepped inside. Rainwater covered the floor in the main room. The water wasn't deep, but it was enough to do serious damage to the floor and drywall. Bottles of hair care products were scattered across the salon, mingling with twigs, broken tree limbs, dried leaves, and small pink curlers. A thick branch of the fallen tree hung through the ceiling above one of the chairs. Looking up, Mel saw the cloudy sky above the large hole in the roof.

"We'd better get a tarp over that before it dumps more rain on us," he said.

"I was thinking the same thing. I'll head over to the hardware store to get a tarp and some rope. We'll need guys with chainsaws, too. I'll put out the word for help."

Mel thought of the expression on Terri's face. "Maybe you should ask Angie to take her home."

"She won't go." Bill shook his head. "Trust me on that. She's tiny, but she's tough. She's had to be."

"What do you mean?"

"She's never had it easy. She lost both parents when she was a teenager. Then she married Vic, who's a classic deadbeat dad. He doesn't pay child support so she's got to financially care for Lyssa on her own. There aren't any living family members for them to lean on in hard times." He made a sweeping motion with his hand. "She took a risk, buying this building, but she made it succeed. Now look at it." He shook his head again. "She's taking it hard, but she'll rally. She always does."

By early afternoon, the rain had passed. Men with chainsaws—under the direction of Larry Tatlock, owner of a local tree service—had cut the broken trunk into sections and stacked the wood in the parking space behind the shop.

At least I'll have plenty of firewood next winter, Terri thought as she carried a plastic garbage bag to the Dumpster in the alley.

Tears threatened, but she swallowed them. She hadn't any time to give in to self-pity. Besides, look at all the people who'd turned out to help as soon as they heard what happened. She was blessed by good friends.

BJ Olson, her insurance agent, had said he would have information for her this afternoon regarding estimates, and Bill Palmer had a friend who was a contractor. Someone else—she didn't remember who—had said he thought she could be working inside her salon again in two or three weeks. It might be inconvenient with some construction continuing, but it would be doable. She hoped he was right.

She tossed the trash bag into the blue Dumpster and turned to face the rear of her building. Hers and the Farmers Independent Bank's building, that is. The monthly mortgage payment for the brick and frame structure wasn't much, all things considered, but neither was her income most months. If she had to close the salon for two weeks or more . . .

Father-God, please let the insurance cover the cost of repairs. And if not, give me the wisdom to know what to do about it.

The Idaho Bureau of Occupational Licenses was strict about how and where a licensed cosmetologist practiced her trade. Otherwise, Terri could have cut hair in her kitchen until the repairs to the salon were finished. But the law wouldn't allow her to do that, and she didn't believe in breaking the law. God would have to show her another way.

Mel Jenkins exited the back door of the building, packing an armload of branches that he'd cleared from the interior of her salon. At some point during the day, he'd changed from business attire into faded Levi's and a blue sweatshirt. It was a good look on him.

He dropped the debris on top of a growing pile

of the same, then brushed dried leaves from the front and sleeves of his sweatshirt. When he turned, he saw her. After a moment's hesitation, he strode forward.

"How're you holding up?"

Oh, those blasted tears! There they were, threatening again. "I'm okay. Thanks." She glanced at her wristwatch. "School will be out soon. I'm not sure Lyssa should be here during the clean-up."

"Why don't you go on home? There isn't anything we're doing that requires you to be here. We'll make sure nothing important gets tossed out."

"I don't know . . ."

"Let Angie drive you home," he said gently. "You're exhausted. You should get some rest."

His image swam before her.

"Hey." His hand alighted on her shoulder. "It's going to be okay."

She choked on a sob.

A heartbeat later, he drew her into his embrace. "It'll be okay." He patted her back. "It'll be okay."

Despite her tears, she smiled a little, sensing his uncertainty. It had been a long while since a man held her in his arms. Had it been as long since Mel held a woman the way he was holding her now?

It took every ounce of Mel's will not to brush the tears from Terri's cheeks with his thumbs and then kiss her quivering lips. He wanted to comfort her. He wished he could draw her closer, hold on tight, not let her go for a long, long while, not until he could make everything better for her.

Except he'd learned that he couldn't always make things better. He couldn't stop people from hurting. Or from dying.

"Life is hard," Mel's mother had often said. "But God is good."

For a time, such comments had made him want to rage. How could a good God allow bad, senseless things to happen? Why did the innocent so often suffer? He'd found no human answers to those questions, but somehow, some way, the rage in his heart had ceased. He'd begun to trust again, trust that the God of heaven had a plan and a purpose in all things.

Terri drew a shuddering breath and stepped back.

"Sorry," she whispered. "I didn't mean to lose it like that."

He wished he could pull her into his embrace a second time. He wished he could comfort her a little while longer. Instead, he said, "It's understandable. You have a tree sitting in your beautician's chair."

That drew a little smile. "You're kind."

"I'm glad I can help." He motioned with his arm toward Municipal Street. "Now, let's have Angie take you home."

7

"Don't you dare cancel," Angie scolded over the telephone the next afternoon.

Terri lay back on her bed, staring at the ceiling. "I don't *feel* like going out."

"Of course you don't, but you need to anyway."

"I won't be a fun date. I'm tired, and I'm worried."

"Mel will understand. And going out will take your mind off the salon for a few hours. You need that. Sometimes escape can be a good thing. Instead of thinking about your building's roof, you can watch Tom Cruise save civilization from the pod people or whatever they are."

Worry churned in Terri's stomach. There was a

wide gap between the early estimate for repair costs and what she thought the insurance policy would cover. BJ had told her to relax, that the adjuster wasn't finished assessing the damage; Terri wasn't doing a good job of following that particular piece of advice.

Fear was the opposite of faith. She knew that. Yet fear persisted. She couldn't keep appointments at her shattered salon, and the law wouldn't allow her to work out of her home without major renovations.

The facts were, no appointments, no income. She had some money in savings, but nowhere near enough. She and Lyssa had never done without any necessity. God had been faithful to provide. But if she couldn't work, what would—

"Terri, are you listening to me?"

"What?" She blinked. "Oh . . . No . . . Sorry."

Angie laughed softly. "I'm taking Lyssa for the night, and *you* are going out to dinner and a movie with Mel. Get used to it. I'll see you about 5:00."

"Okay. Okay."

"That's a little over an hour from now."

"I know. Lyssa will be ready for you."

"And you need to get ready, too. You know what I mean. Do something with your hair. Put on some makeup."

"Yeah, yeah, yeah. All right. Quit nagging."

They said good-bye, and Terri hung up the phone.

She could have told Angie it wasn't *that* kind of date. She liked Mel, but it wasn't as if she expected fireworks. They barely knew each other. Besides, now wasn't a good time for her to contemplate romance. Not with her salon wrecked and her money worries. No, she and Mel would probably end up as friends, and that would be fine with her. A person could never have too many friends.

She rose from the bed and crossed the room to the closet, feeling better now that her expectations for the evening had been set in order.

"Wear that sweater you got in the mail, Mom."

Terri glanced over her shoulder to look at Lyssa striding into the bedroom, holding a small bag of chips in her left hand.

"That one there." Her daughter pointed to the soft teal sweater Terri had received from a catalog order a couple of weeks before. "It's almost the same color as your eyes."

Terri pulled the sweater, tags still attached, from the shelf in her closet, shook it out, then held it in front of her as she turned to look at her reflection in the mirror. She shouldn't wear it. She should return it for a refund. Money would be tight for a long while to come. She needed to save and cut corners every way she could. She had plenty of sweaters already, and summer would be here soon. She wouldn't need her sweaters then.

"Mr. Jenkins thinks you're pretty, Mom."

"Does he?" She felt a flutter of unanticipated pleasure.

"Sure." Lyssa hopped on to her mother's bed and pretzeled her legs. "'Cause you are. Everybody thinks so."

"I doubt everybody does. You do because you're prejudiced."

"What's that?"

"Prejudiced?" She sank onto the bed beside her daughter. "It means you're predisposed to be biased for or against something."

The frown on Lyssa's forehead told Terri the definition hadn't clarified the meaning.

She ruffled her daughter's hair with one hand, then stroked her cheek. "You see me as pretty because you love me, because I'm your mom, not because of how I really look."

Lyssa's mouth pursed and her eyes narrowed. "Nope," she said after a lengthy pause, her smile returning. "I think you're pretty 'cause you are."

As she rose from the bed, Terri smiled briefly, knowing she wouldn't change her daughter's mind and glad of it. She walked to the mirror and held the blue-green sweater against her torso. Lyssa was right. It was a close match to the color of her eyes. She supposed it wouldn't hurt to keep it. It hadn't been all that expensive.

A wave of panic hit her like an unexpected punch in the stomach. *God, how will we manage until the salon can reopen?* The room seemed to sway, and her stomach hurt.

"Mom, I like Mr. Jenkins. He's really nice."

I've got enough money in the bank to make the next mortgage payment. But how long will it be before I can work again? What if my clients go elsewhere? What if I can't get them back once I reopen? They might find someone they like better. How much will I need to borrow to make the repairs? I don't know if my credit is good enough for what I'll need. If it isn't . . .

She lowered her gaze from the mirror, unable to look at her reflection any longer.

"You like the coach, too. Right, Mom?"

She shook her head from side to side, not listening to her daughter as a litany of her problems—existing and potential—played in her mind.

After leaving her mom to get dressed, Lyssa went into her bedroom and closed the door. She sank onto the floor near the built-in shelves that held her most prized possessions—her various sports trophies, an autographed baseball, a collection of stuffed teddy bears and Breyer horses, her favorite books.

She felt awful. She'd heard her mom talking on the phone, saying she didn't want to go out with Coach Jenkins tonight. Her mom didn't like the coach after all. She was unhappy, and it was Lyssa's fault. If Lyssa hadn't tricked the coach into winning the cake at the carnival, then he wouldn't have asked her mom to go to the movies with him; and if her mom hadn't agreed to go, then she wouldn't be sad now.

Lyssa should've told her mom she didn't have to go anywhere with the coach. She didn't want to be a starting pitcher badly enough to make her mom do something she didn't want to do, something that made her miserable. Besides, Coach had said Lyssa wasn't ready yet. She shouldn't be so impatient. Worse, she shouldn't be so selfish. And she never should've lied about the number she pulled out of the bowl at the cakewalk.

"Dear Jesus, please don't let my mom be unhappy. I'm sorry for what I did. Really sorry. I'll make it up to her somehow. I promise."

Two thoughts crossed Mel's mind when Terri opened the door for him: she looked tired—understandable, considering what had happened to her salon yesterday—and she looked beautiful. How she managed to do both at the same time amazed him.

"How's it going?"

She gave a slight shrug. "Okay."

He might not know her as well as he hoped to, but he knew her well enough to recognize the worry in her eyes. Maybe he should tell her they didn't have to—

"Let me grab my purse and coat, and we can go."

Minutes later, they were in his car, headed for the Over the Rainbow Diner. Mel had considered taking Terri to a nicer restaurant up at the resort or down in Twin Falls, but something had told him it was best to keep this first date simple and casual.

Simple and casual . . . but maybe it shouldn't be dead silent.

He cleared his throat. "Is Lyssa ready for our practice tomorrow? We've got lots to work on before the season opener."

"She's always ready to play baseball. Practice or an actual game, she loves it. She has since she was about four years old. Instead of *Sesame Street*, she wanted to watch baseball games on ESPN."

"She's a good kid. I've enjoyed coaching her." He glanced to his right. In the glow of the streetlights, he saw Terri smile as she stared out the front windshield.

"She *is* a good kid." The simple words were laced with a mother's love.

"Does Lyssa remember her dad?"

Terri didn't reply.

"Sorry." His grip tightened on the steering wheel. "That's none of my business."

"No. It's okay. I guess I assume everybody in Hart's Crossing already knows the whole pitiful story."

"We don't have to—"

"I don't mind talking about it, Mel." She laughed softly. "And isn't that why we're going out? So we can get to know each other better and become friends?"

Mel hoped they would become more than friends, but he kept that to himself.

"First dates are awkward, aren't they?" Terri added.

He chuckled. "Can't say I remember. I haven't been on a first date in years." He felt her looking at him but kept his gaze on the road.

"I suppose that's something you should tell me about."

He supposed so, too.

"In answer to your question," Terri said, "Lyssa's dad doesn't see her. After he moved away, he broke off all contact, with me and with his daughter. Lyssa was a toddler when Vic left, so she doesn't remember him. That makes things a little easier, I suppose." She paused before adding, "But not having a dad leaves a void in her life, all the same. Every little girl wants a dad to love and to love her back."

Mel wondered if Terri felt a void in her life, too. "Must have been rough for you both."

"Hard enough." Another pause. "But the Lord sustains us."

A number of follow-up questions filled Mel's head, but he had no time to ask them before he pulled into a parking space not far from the diner.

Seated in the rear booth at the Over the Rainbow Diner, red baskets of Tin Man Fish and Chips and tall glasses of Diet Coke on the table between them, Terri found herself relaxing in Mel's company. He made her feel comfortable, as if she'd known him all of her life. Perhaps it was the gentle tone of his voice or the way he leaned forward whenever she spoke, as if he didn't want to miss a single word she said. Being with him made her forget her worries about the salon and the insurance and her too-low bank account balance.

Responding to his questions, she told him more about the end of her marriage after Vic left town with another woman. She shared the challenges of being a single mom, but she also talked about the joys of motherhood and Lyssa's dreams of playing in the Little League World Series.

She felt her cheeks grow warm when she realized how long she'd talked about herself. She couldn't remember the last time someone had plied so much information out of her at one sitting.

She took a quick sip of her cola. "Now it's your turn. Tell me about yourself. What brought you to Hart's Crossing?"

"Besides my job?"

She nodded.

"I lost someone, too. I was engaged to be married. We'd been planning the wedding for months when my fiancée passed away suddenly. She was sick only a short time. No one realized she was that ill. Not me. Not her parents."

"I'm sorry."

Mel nodded, acknowledging her sympathy. "I shut down for a long time. I was angry at God and felt cheated by life. I took the job in Hart's Crossing so I could get away from all the memories that lurked around every corner in our hometown. You know how that is."

"Yes."

"It's a wonder God didn't give up on me."

He smiled gently, and Terri saw peace in his eyes. A deep kind of peace that came with trusting God. She returned the smile, feeling a kinship with him. A kinship of loss. A kinship of faith.

"I'm glad I came to Hart's Crossing," he said, his gaze locked with hers.

Me, too.

After a lengthy silence, Terri lowered her eyes, not wanting Mel to see her jumbled emotions. She wasn't as relaxed as she'd been minutes before, but she was not relaxed in a good way. In a way she hadn't experienced in years. In a heart-fluttering, this-can't-be-happening-to-me sort of way.

It was then she looked at her wristwatch and realized how long they'd been in the diner. "We missed the start of the first movie, didn't we?"

A crooked smile lifted one corner of his mouth higher than the other. "Yeah."

"I'm sorry. I—"

"I'm not." The smile slowly faded. His blue gaze was intense.

Terri remembered the feel of his arms around her yesterday. She'd thought the embrace a bit awkward at the time, but now she recalled the breadth of his shoulders and the strength of his biceps as he wrapped her close.

"Mr. Jenkins thinks you're pretty, Mom."

Mel's crooked smile returned, as if he'd read Terri's thoughts. Heat rose up her neck and flowed into her cheeks once again, and she longed for the darkness of the theater where she could hide her embarrassment.

"Come on." Mel slid to his feet beside the booth. "I'll bet we haven't missed anything but commercials and previews." He offered his hand.

She reached for it, amazed by how right it felt, her smaller hand enfolded within his larger one—and she completely forgot that Mel Jenkins was expected to become a good friend and nothing more.

8

The telephone rang shortly after 8:00 the next morning. Terri knew the time only because she had to open her eyes to find the noisy instrument.

"Hello," she said, her voice gravelly with sleep.

"You're not up?" Angie laughed. "Must've been a late night."

Terri closed her eyes again. "Late for me. We got to my place around 11:30."

"And?"

She smiled. "We had a good time, Miss Nosey."

"Oh, I knew you would. I just knew it." In a soft, wheedling tone, Angie asked, "Did he kiss you good night?"

"No, but it was only our first date." What Terri

didn't tell her friend was that she'd been disappointed when he didn't *try* to kiss her. She'd thought he might. She'd hoped he would.

"So, what's on your plate today?"

Terri groaned. "More cleaning up at the salon. I've got a contractor coming to look at it on Monday morning so I want to be ready for him. And Lyssa's got her baseball practice this afternoon. It's the last one before the opening game."

"Listen, you take care of business at the shop, and I'll take Lyssa to her practice and stay until you get there."

"I can't ask you to do that, Ang."

"You're not asking. I'm offering."

"Are you sure?"

"I'm sure. It's going to be a lovely day. I can sit in the bleachers and work on my laptop."

"What are you writing now?"

"Nothing creative, if that's what you mean. I'm making long lists of things I must accomplish before the wedding." She laughed. "It seems that's all I've been doing from the moment Bill proposed. I didn't know planning a wedding took so much time. There's always something new to add to the list, something I didn't anticipate."

Terri smiled as she slid up against the headboard. "Don't forget to enjoy yourself, too."

"Good advice. And don't *you* forget that we're driving down to Twin on Monday as soon as school's out to look at bridesmaid dresses for you and Lyssa."

Terri winced. Was that this Monday?

"I know you've got lots of other things on your mind, Terri, but you can still go, can't you? We don't want to put this off too long. Finding the right gowns can be hard."

"Yes. Of course Lyssa and I can go." She hoped the contractor would be done long before then.

Lyssa had lain awake in the middle of the night, staring at the ceiling of Angie's guest room, trying to figure out how to fix the mess she'd caused. She didn't want to tell her mom how she'd lied about the number she drew out of the bowl at the carnival.

Well, she hadn't looked at the scrap of paper, so she didn't know for *sure* it was a lie.

Only something in her heart told her it was the

same thing. She'd told Jesus she was sorry, but now she needed to fix it so her mom wasn't unhappy about the coach.

When she'd asked her mom if she liked him, Lyssa hadn't expected her to shake her head no. Why didn't her mom like him? He was nice. Lyssa liked him a lot.

But she loved her mom even more, and she'd do just about anything to make her mom happy. She would even give up playing in a Little League World Series if that's what it took.

Of course, if she didn't get to pitch much for the Cavaliers, that would never happen anyway.

Mel whistled as he reached into the back of his pickup for the oversized box that held bats, balls, and a few extra gloves. He hadn't felt this good in ages—and that was thanks to a pretty redhead with blue-green eyes and a sad-sweet smile that made his heart race.

"Good afternoon, Mr. Jenkins."

Leaving the box on the tailgate, he turned around. Till Hart walked toward him, clad in a bright pink warm-up suit, athletic shoes, and a sun visor. "Afternoon, Miss Hart. Nice day for a walk."

"Yes, indeedy." She glanced up at the cloudless sky, then back at him. "Getting ready for practice, I see."

"Yes, ma'am."

"If you don't mind, I'll sit and watch a spell."

"I don't mind, but the team won't start arriving for another half hour or so." Wrapping his arms around the box, he pulled it against his chest and lifted it off the tailgate.

"Well, then, you and I can have us a chat while we wait for them."

"Sounds good." He started walking toward the baseball diamond, shortening his stride to accommodate the older woman.

"I'm told you and Terri Sampson had dinner together last night."

Mel chuckled as he looked at Till. "I think that made the rounds quicker than the news of Bill and Angie's engagement."

"If you'd wanted it to be a secret, you wouldn't have taken Terri to the diner." She winked at him, but when she continued, her tone was somber. "I hope you managed to cheer her spirits some. Such a shame what happened to her salon."

Mel set the box on the lower bench of the metal bleachers. "She'll bounce back." *And if she'll let me, I'll help her do it.*

"I know she will. Terri's made of sterner stuff." Till settled onto the second row. "More importantly, she puts her trust in Christ. Knowing the Lord makes the burdens easier to carry."

"Yes," he agreed softly. "It does."

Till gave her head a nod, and Mel had the feeling he'd passed some sort of test.

"By the way, Mr. Jenkins, I have an idea for where Terri might do hair until her salon is repaired. There's a—"

The crunch of tires on gravel drew both of their gazes toward the parking lot. A cloud of dust settled as the driver and passenger doors opened, releasing Angie Hunter and Lyssa Sampson.

Mel swallowed his disappointment. He'd looked forward to seeing Terri this afternoon.

"Hello, Miss Hart," Lyssa called. "You gonna watch the practice?"

"I thought I might."

Mel said, "I could use your help, Lyssa."

"Okay." She seemed a little reluctant as she walked toward him, her cap pulled low on her forehead. "What d'you want me to do?"

"Let's get these out." He handed her one of the white rubber bases. "You take third. I'll take first and second."

"Sure." She turned and ran down the baseline toward third.

Mel took the other two bases and strode toward first. By the time he reached second, Lyssa was there.

She met his gaze briefly, then looked up and studied the sky. "So how was the movie last night?"

Mel knelt to fasten the base in place. "Pretty good."

"I heard it's kind of creepy. Were you scared?"

"No." He shook his head. "I wasn't scared." He smiled to himself. "But I think your mom was a few times."

107

Lyssa was silent awhile before saying, "Most of Mom's boyfriends take her dancing and to dress-up places like that. She likes doin' that kind of fancy stuff better than going to the Apollo."

Most of her boyfriends? Dancing? He'd gotten the impression Terri didn't go out much.

"She thinks scary movies like *War of the Worlds* are dumb."

Mel sat back on his heels and looked at Lyssa. "She seemed to enjoy herself last night."

"Yeah, well." Lyssa shrugged. "Mom was trying to be nice to you. You know. She didn't want to hurt your feelings. Do unto others and stuff like that." A touch of pink painted her cheeks as she lowered her gaze to the ground. "I'll go get the bats out." She took off at a run, straight across the pitcher's mound.

"She was being *nice* to me?"

Had he misread Terri? He'd thought she enjoyed herself last night. He'd believed something good was happening between them. Sure, the sci-fi movies were just okay, but the dinner had gone great. At least, he'd thought so. He'd liked listening to her talk about her life and about Lyssa. When she spoke of her ex-husband, there hadn't been any signs of bitterness. Even in her concern about her beauty salon, she'd carried a spirit of hope in her voice and in her eyes. He suspected her faith ran deep, as Till Hart said.

He looked toward the bleachers where Angie sat beside Till, the two of them engrossed in conversation.

Why had Angie brought Lyssa to baseball practice? Was Terri avoiding him? He hadn't dated in a long time, but he'd thought he could read women better than that.

A cloud seemed to fall across the sunny day as Mel stood and walked across the baseball field toward home plate.

Terri placed a hand in the small of her spine and arched backward, a groan escaping her lips. It surprised her, how much damage rainwater and wind could do. But she was done with her salvaging. When the contractor showed up on Monday, she would be ready for him. God willing, he wouldn't be tied up with another job that would delay him starting on hers soon.

Her cell phone vibrated in her pocket. She grabbed it, saw Angie's number in the ID, and flipped it open. "Hey, Ang."

"What happened to you? Don't tell me you're still at the salon."

"I just finished up. I should be over to the field in five minutes. Ten tops."

"Don't bother. Practice is over. The kids are clearing out."

Terri looked at the wall, but the clock was no longer there. It had fallen victim to the storm. Her gaze dropped to her wristwatch. "I didn't know it was this late. I'm sorry, Angie. I never meant for you to stay with Lyssa the whole day."

"To tell the truth, I enjoyed it. Who'd have thought I'd become a fan of Little League baseball?"

Terri laughed, remembering the first Cavalier game Angie attended, shortly after her return to Hart's Crossing. She hadn't liked the cold weather or the noise made by the spectators, and she definitely hadn't understood how a Little League team's victory over their arch rivals could cause an entire town to celebrate.

Angie's voice lowered almost to a whisper. "There's something you should know, Terri. I think Lyssa's had a falling out with Mel."

"What do you mean?"

"I'm not sure. It's a feeling I've got." There was a moment of silence, then she added, "Here comes Lyssa. Looks like she's ready to go. Want me to bring her to the shop or take her home?"

"Home, thanks. I'll lock up now and meet you there."

"Okay. See you soon."

Terri frowned as she closed the cell phone. Why would Angie think Lyssa and Mel were at odds? Had he criticized her pitching? Had he left her off the play roster for opening day? Lyssa wasn't prone to pouting, but she could be stubborn, especially when it came to baseball.

Well, Terri wouldn't know if a problem existed until she talked to Lyssa. It was probably nothing. Angie didn't have children of her own, so she most likely misread something in Lyssa's behavior.

Terri slipped the phone into her pocket and headed for the rear door of the salon.

*Most of her boyfriends . . . She'd rather go dancing
. . . Just being nice to me . . .*

Mel sat in his truck in the empty parking lot and
dialed Terri's number. The phone rang numerous
times before the answering machine finally picked
up. As soon as the beep sounded, he said, "Terri,
it's Mel. Sorry you didn't make it to Lyssa's practice.
Hope nothing's wrong. I'll . . . ah . . . I'll give you
a call later."

After flipping the cell phone closed, he stared
at it. Maybe he should have asked her to call him
back when she had time. Then the ball would have
been in her court, not his. If she wasn't interested,
she should say so. Right?

He felt stupid. How could he have misread her
that way? But maybe he hadn't. Maybe Lyssa was the
one who was wrong. Still, Lyssa didn't seem like the
kind of kid to misunderstand what her mom had
said, and Terri must have said something or where
else would Lyssa have gotten the notion her mom
was only being nice to him? Whatever Terri had said
couldn't have been good.

"Do unto others and stuff like that." Lyssa's words

still stung. A ten-year-old didn't think up that phrase on her own. Either Terri had said it to her, or Lyssa had overheard her mom saying it to someone else. No matter which, he felt like an idiot.

What had he been thinking, wanting to get involved in a relationship again? Especially with a divorced woman and her daughter. It was safer to keep to himself.

It was suppertime before Terri broached the subject of the coach with Lyssa. One reason she waited was because Lyssa had homework to finish, but she also waited because she'd hoped Mel would call again as he'd said he would in the message left on her answering machine.

But he didn't call again.

"I'm sorry I didn't make your practice game," Terri said as she passed the bowl of fluffy mashed potatoes to Lyssa.

"It's okay." Her daughter shrugged. "It was only a practice."

"Did Mr. Jenkins have you pitch?"

Lyssa hooked a loose strand of strawberry-blond

hair behind her ear before putting two scoops of potatoes on her plate. "Yeah, I pitched a couple of innings."

"Was the coach pleased with your game?"

"I guess." She sounded listless. Very unlike herself.

"Lyssa, is something wrong between you and Mr. Jenkins?"

"Me and the coach?" Lyssa shook her head, her gaze fastened to her supper plate. "No," she mumbled.

"Honey?" Terri was getting concerned now. "Tell me what's wrong."

"I don't know. It just feels . . . weird. You know. To have you and the coach . . . you know." Her daughter wrinkled her nose. "Dating."

"But I thought you liked him. I thought you wanted me to go out with him."

"I do like him, Mom. But—" Lyssa looked up at last. "I don't think he oughta be your boyfriend. Do *you?*" Her question rose on an anxious note, as if the idea caused her pain.

Terri lifted the bowl of corn and passed it to her daughter. "I suppose not." *Not if it makes you un-*

happy. She swallowed a sigh. *Not if he doesn't call and ask me out again.*

"I didn't think so."

Neither one of them said much more as they ate their supper.

9

Terri didn't sleep well that night. She tossed and turned, tossed and turned, her thoughts racing.

It shouldn't bother her this much, that Lyssa didn't want her to see Mel Jenkins socially. After all, they'd only had one date, and he hadn't even kissed her.

Besides, Terri had seen the sort of problems that came with step-parenting. Blended families were no piece of cake to make work. Mel was good with the kids on the team, but was he the right kind of man for a stepdad?

Stepdad? What was she thinking? Why worry about blended families after one date? Besides, maybe she was wrong to want to marry again. She hadn't exactly chosen well the first time around.

How could she know she would choose better if given another chance?

Yet there was something about Mel that drew her to him. She wanted to know him more, better. He was gentle, yet strong. Nice looking, but not full of himself. Sometimes he was funny, other times serious. He was intelligent and had a responsible position with the bank. The kids he coached liked him. Lyssa liked him. Terri had witnessed his caring patience with them. He was a man of faith, a faith that had been tested by the loss of his fiancée and come out stronger on the other side.

She pulled the pillow from behind her head and placed it over her face.

Hadn't she enough to worry about? She had a building in disrepair, a home to run, a living to earn, a daughter to raise. Why complicate her life with a man? She should remember that marriage wasn't always happy and romantic. Even when two people loved each other, there was stress and strain involved. And if Lyssa didn't want her to date Mel, that was enough reason to keep her distance.

Wasn't it?

So what am I going to do?

Mel stared at his reflection in the bathroom mirror, his razor held close to his lathered jaw.

He should have called Terri again last night, like he'd said he would in his message. Why hadn't he?

Because he was a coward. Because he was afraid he would find out Lyssa had told the truth. Because he cared for Terri Sampson more than he should after only one date. Because he didn't want to discover that she didn't feel the same about him.

Worry about nothing. Pray about everything. That's the advice he would give someone else in his shoes. Maybe it wouldn't hurt to practice some of it himself.

"Terri," Till Hart called from a corner of the narthex as church members exited the sanctuary.

Terri waved to acknowledge she'd heard her, then made her way through the crowd of folks. "How are you, Miss Hart?"

"Fine and dandy, thanks. Do you have time to do something with me?"

When Terri got home, she would probably start

mulling over the same thoughts she'd had during the night. Any distraction from that would be welcome. "Of course, Miss Hart. What do you need?"

"It's about your hair business."

"My salon?"

"Mr. Palmer tells me it will take some time before you're able to get back into your building."

"I'm afraid that's true."

"Well, I have found a place for you. My friend has a basement room that is perfect, and she's agreed to let you use it."

"Oh, Miss Hart. That's very kind. But the state of Idaho has very strict laws regarding square footage and separate entrances and—"

Till waved a hand in dismissal. "Yes, yes. I've been told all that, and that's just what I've found for you. Could you drive me over to Willow Lane so I can show you? I promise not to keep you from your Sunday dinner more than an hour."

Terri saw no polite way out of it. "Of course. I'll be glad to drive you anywhere you wish."

Home from church, Mel sat at his kitchen table,

staring at the portable phone, debating whether or not to call Terri.

He hadn't heard much of Reverend Ball's sermon, although it probably was a fine one. The minister might be retirement age, but he still knew how to deliver a powerful message. However, Mel's thoughts had been focused on a woman and her daughter who lived in a small, two-story house, not on the good reverend's words.

Lord, what's the answer? Should I call her or not? Do you mean for us to be together? Is this in your will? I know you wanted me to leave the mourning behind, to start living again. But have I made a major blunder with Terri?

She couldn't believe her eyes. The well-lit basement had a stylist chair, a shampoo bowl, two large mirrors, shelves for supplies, even an outside entrance with a ramp for wheelchair access. The style of the furnishings was straight out of the 1960's, but everything looked in pristine condition except for a layer of dust.

"Why didn't I know you were a cosmetologist, Mrs. Osborn?"

Elizabeth Osborn, a woman in her late seventies with an impeccably coifed head of snow-white hair, laughed softly. "It's been almost twenty years since I closed my salon, dear girl. There's no reason you should have known."

"You're sure you wouldn't mind me using it?"

"Of course, I wouldn't mind. I'd be delighted. Think of the people who'll come to see you for an appointment and then they might stop upstairs to say hello to me, too. I don't get around as well as I used to. My bad hip, you know. I miss the company." She patted her hair. "Besides, I'd hate to see your clients go to Mary Lou Hitchens out on the highway. That woman couldn't find her way around a perm rod to save her soul."

Terri subdued a laugh before asking the inevitable. "About the rent?"

"Oh, goodness gracious. I don't need a thing."

"I insist, Mrs. Osborn. I'd be using your power and heat and water. I must pay something. I could be here for a month."

"I'll tell you what. I know a woman who leases a station down in Twin Falls. I'll ask what she pays for rent in that salon she's in, then we'll come up with something reasonable for this location and the service provided. How does that sound?"

"It sounds more than fair." Terri grinned as some of her money worries slid off her shoulders.

And if God could take care of the detail of finding her a place to work while Terri's Tangles was restored, surely he would take care of other things in her future as well. Things such as her feelings about Mel Jenkins.

Mel got Terri's answering machine again. It made him wonder if she was screening her calls in order to avoid him. Frustrated, he hung up without leaving a message.

10

"That's it!" Angie exclaimed. "That's the one."

Terri stood in the oversized dressing room at Baskins Formal and Bridal in Twin Falls, looking into the floor-to-ceiling mirror. The tea-length matte satin dress was a shade of mossy green that the sales-clerk had called celadon. It had off-the-shoulder sleeves and a modest neckline. The cut was simple, the style classic.

"That's a dress you could wear out. It doesn't look like a bridesmaid dress that you wear once and hang in your closet. You know what I mean?" Angie said.

"I know what you mean. But I don't know where I'd wear it. Too dressy for church."

Angie tilted her head slightly to one side, meeting Terri's gaze in the mirror. "I meant on a date, silly."

"Hmm."

"What's up?" Angie stood and stepped to Terri's side. "Something's bothering you."

Terri listened to Lyssa's muffled chattering with Angie's mom in another dressing room. Francine Hunter had graciously taken Lyssa and about a dozen different dresses into that room a short while before.

"Can't you tell me?" Angie asked.

"It's Mel . . . and Lyssa." *And me.*

"So I was right about Saturday? Lyssa had a falling out with him."

"Not exactly. Well, not that I know of, anyway."

Once Terri got started, the words tumbled out in a rush. She told Angie how much she'd enjoyed her date with Mel, how she hadn't expected to like him so much, how disappointed she'd been when Lyssa said she didn't want Terri to have Mel as a boyfriend, how awful it made her feel that he hadn't called again. By the time she finished, she was holding a tissue to her nose and hoping she wouldn't stain the bridesmaid dress with her tears.

Angie was silent as she helped Terri out of the satin gown and returned it to its padded hanger. It wasn't until the two were seated side by side on the bench in the dressing room, Terri wrapped in a soft robe provided by the dress shop, that Angie said, "If you like him so much, is it a good thing to allow your ten-year-old daughter to determine your future? Shouldn't that be something you let God decide?"

The question brought her up short.

Angie took hold of one of Terri's hands. "Have you had a heart-to-heart with Lyssa to find out what happened?"

"No."

"Don't you think it's time you did?"

Terri sniffed and wiped her eyes again. "Yes. I think it is."

Mel was seated on the sofa, watching the evening news on television, when a voice in his head said, *What are you waiting for? Get over there and talk to her.*

This time, he didn't second-guess himself. He

got up, put on his coat, and headed for the garage, truck keys in hand.

Terri and Lyssa had been home from Twin Falls about an hour when Terri tapped on Lyssa's bedroom door, waited a moment, then cracked it open. "Sweetheart?"

Her daughter sat cross-legged on her bed, headphones plugging her ears and CD player in hand. Even from the doorway, Terri could hear the music pounding away.

Raising her voice, she asked, "May I come in?"

Startled, Lyssa looked up. After a moment's hesitation, she pressed the stop button on the CD player and removed the headphones.

"Lyssa, we need to talk."

"About what?"

"About Mr. Jenkins."

Tears pooled in her daughter's eyes. "I'm sorry, Mom."

"Sorry for what?" Terri moved to the bed and sat down beside Lyssa.

"I didn't mean to lie to you or Mr. Jenkins. It just

sorta happened. I thought if the coach liked your cake, then maybe he'd notice me more and not just think of me as a girl, and he'd give me a chance to start a game." Tears rolled down Lyssa's cheeks as the words tumbled from her lips with ever-increasing speed. "Then when he liked you, I kinda thought that was even better 'cause I like him, too, but then you were unhappy and didn't want to go out with him, and I knew it was all my fault 'cause I lied. I don't know what the number was on that piece of paper at the cakewalk. I just said it was his so he'd get the cake, and then I told another lie so he wouldn't ask you out again. I never meant to lie, but I did. I'm so sorry, Mom."

"I know. I know." Terri took hold of Lyssa's hand. "But honey, what made you think I didn't want to go out with Mr. Jenkins?"

Tears glittered in her daughter's eyes. "I heard you tell Angie you didn't want to go out with him."

Terri tried to remember when she'd said any such thing.

"You looked so sad, Mom, and it was all my fault." Lyssa released a tiny sob.

Understanding began to dawn.

"Shh." She drew her daughter into her arms. "Sweetheart, whatever it was you did or said, I love you. Nothing will change that. We'll sort this out, the two of us. Okay?"

Lyssa sniffed and uttered a muffled, "Okay."

Smiling as she held Lyssa close, Terri felt a glimmer of hope in her heart.

Mel forced himself to observe the speed limit as he followed the tree-lined streets. When he arrived at the Sampson home, he stopped his truck next to the curb and killed the engine, then took a deep breath.

"Father, give me the right words to say when I see her," he whispered. "I can't do this without you."

He got out of the truck, rounded the cab, and came to a halt on the sidewalk. Staring at the front of the house, he folded his arms over his chest and took another deep breath. Maybe he should have rehearsed what he meant to say before he came over.

Help me, Lord.

After another steadying breath, he strode up the walk and rang the doorbell. It seemed forever before the door opened.

Surprise—and an emotion Mel couldn't define—flickered in Terri's eyes. "Mel," she said softly.

"Terri. Listen, I'm sorry for not calling again."

She acknowledged his apology with a nod.

"I tried to call, but you didn't answer." He pushed away the doubt as he cleared his throat. "I . . . uh . . . I'm not quite sure how to say this."

She seemed willing to wait for him to figure it out.

"Terri, I like you. A lot. I enjoyed being with you Friday night. I was hoping . . . well, I hoped we might see more of each other. I felt something with you that I haven't felt in a long while. But Lyssa said you—"

"Mel, she was wrong."

His heart thrummed with sudden hope. "She was?"

"Yes." A slight smile curved the corners of her mouth. "I'd like to spend time with you, too." She glanced over her shoulder toward the stairs, then back at him. "Won't you come in and sit down? I have a story to tell you about a girl, a chocolate cake, and Little League baseball."

Faith, the Bible said, was being sure of what he hoped for and certain of what he didn't see. As Mel looked into Terri's eyes, his heart told him that he needed to have some of that faith now—and let God work.

Epilogue

Lyssa wrinkled her nose as Bill Palmer fed his bride a piece of wedding cake, then kissed her with the frosting still on her lips.

But it wasn't the kiss that bothered Lyssa. It was this silly dress she wore. The lace around her neck was scratchy, and the satin fabric felt funny against her skin, all clingy and slick. Besides, it made her look like a dork.

While the photographer snapped more pictures of the bride and groom, Lyssa turned away, her gaze scanning the church's fellowship hall. The place was packed with people standing and sitting everywhere.

It seemed like the whole town had turned out to see Angie Hunter and Bill Palmer get married.

Lyssa thought weddings were okay, but baseball was a whole lot better. Good thing this wedding fell on one of the Cavaliers' free game days or she would have been really upset. Especially since her team was on a major winning streak.

Through the crowd of wedding guests, Lyssa saw her mom. Mom didn't look like a dork in her satin dress. She looked like a princess. Her whole face sparkled with happiness.

And the coach, who stood close to her mom, talking and smiling, looked pretty good in his fancy suit, too. Almost like the Prince Charming her mom said she used to hope and pray for.

Sometimes, grownups were weird.

A sneak peek at
Book 4 of the Hart's Crossing series
Sweet Dreams Drive

Soft mewling sounds awakened Patti at 3:00 a.m. She lay still, pretending to be asleep, hoping Al would get up first. Trouble was, if she waited too long, one baby would wake the other, and soon both would be crying.

She heard Al's breathing, a sound not quite a snore, but close enough to it.

As she slipped from beneath the sheet and light-weight blanket, Patti felt a spark of irritation. Not at their precious twins, but at her husband. Why did he get to sleep when she didn't? Didn't he real-ize how exhausted she was? Did he have a clue how hard she worked every day and how little she'd slept in the four weeks since she gave birth?

The two bassinets—one pink, one blue—were set in the far corner of the master bedroom. Moonlight, falling through the open window, illuminated her way across the room. Placing one hand on each bassinet, she leaned over to see which baby was fussing. Like his father, Weston didn't budge. Yvonne, however, punched the air with tiny fists, warming up for a good cry.

"Shh," Patti whispered as she lifted her infant daughter into her arms. "Mommy's here. Shh."

A short while later, as the baby sucked on a bottle of warmed formula, Patti set the rocking chair in motion and stared out the window of the family room. Silvery-white moonlight bathed the rooftop of the house across the back fence. Somewhere in the neighborhood, a dog barked. Soon another dog replied. It was a strangely comforting sound.

She and Al had purchased their home in this new subdivision on the east side of Hart's Crossing last spring. She'd fallen in love with it the moment she entered through the front door. If they were going to stay in this small town, then this was the home she wanted to live in. Yes, the mortgage was higher than what they'd wanted, but whose wasn't? At least they were investing their money instead of throwing it away on rent. She just wished there was a little more of Al's paycheck left over each month after they paid their bills.

She leaned her head against the back of the rocker and closed her eyes as the memory of their latest argument played through her head.

"We could move to a bigger city, Al. You'd make more money in a larger school district."

"I don't want to move. You know that. I want our kids to grow up in Hart's Crossing. Besides, I like my job. I like the people I work with. And our families are here. There's more to life than money, Patti."

"Raising children is expensive. Have you seen the doctor and hospital bills?"

"We'll manage."

Tears spilled from beneath her eyelids, trailing down her cheeks. She and Al never used to fight. Now they seemed to disagree about everything. Her mother said it was whacked-out hormones and too little sleep. Patti didn't know if that was true or not.

But she did wonder if this was the way marriage was supposed to be.

Robin Lee Hatcher discovered her vocation as a novelist after many years of reading everything she could put her hands on, including the backs of cereal boxes and ketchup bottles. However, she's certain there are better plots and fewer calories in her books than in puffed rice and hamburgers.

The winner of numerous writing awards, including the Christy Award for Excellence in Christian Fiction, the RITA Award for Best Inspirational Romance, and RWA's Lifetime Achievement Award, Robin is the author of over forty-five novels, including *Catching Katie*, which was named one of the Best Books of 2004 by the Library Journal.

Robin enjoys being with her family, spending time in the beautiful Idaho outdoors, reading books that make her cry, and watching romantic movies. She is passionate about the theater, and several nights every summer she can be found at the outdoor amphitheater of the Idaho Shakespeare Festival, enjoying Shakespeare under the stars. She makes her home in Boise, sharing it with her dogs, including Poppet the Papillon, also known as "Robin's obsession."

Watch for more news from

HART'S CROSSING
the small town with the big heart